This book belongs to

I2na

How many Fairy Animals books have you collected?

- Chloe the Kitten
- Bella the Bunny
- Paddy the Puppy
- Mia the Mouse
- Poppy the Pony
- Hailey the Hedgehog
- Sophie the Squirrel
- Daisy the Deer
- Kylie the Kitten
- Paige the Pony
- Penny the Puppy
- ✓ Bailey the Bunny

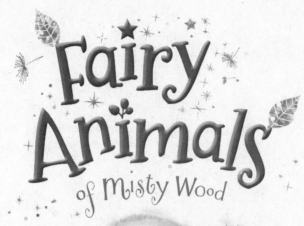

Fairy Animals
of Misty Wood

Bailey the Bunny

Lily Small

Henry Holt and Company
New York

With special thanks to Susannah Leigh

Henry Holt and Company, *Publishers since 1866*
Henry Holt® is a registered trademark of Macmillan Publishing Group, LLC.
175 Fifth Avenue, New York, NY 10010
mackids.com

First published in the United States in 2018 by Henry Holt and Company.
Originally published in Great Britain in 2014 by Egmont UK Limited.

Library of Congress Control Number: 2017945037
ISBN 978-1-250-12704-4

Our books may be purchased in bulk for promotional, educational, or business use.
Please contact your local bookseller or the Macmillan Corporate
and Premium Sales Department at (800) 221-7945 ext. 5442
or by e-mail at MacmillanSpecialMarkets@macmillan.com.

First American edition, 2018
Printed in the United States of America
by LSC Communications, Harrisonburg, Virginia

1 3 5 7 9 10 8 6 4 2

Contents

CHAPTER ONE

A Breakfast Surprise

Spring had come to Misty Wood.
The icy frosts of winter had melted
away and the earth was warm and
bouncy again. On the hillsides,

1

the sweet scent of lavender drifted gently on the breeze. Soft clover carpeted the valleys, and in the meadows, hundreds of new flowers were just ready to bloom.

Below a cluster of mulberry bushes, in a cozy burrow deep inside the Misty Wood Rabbit Warren, somebody was bursting with happiness.

". . . and then I'll twitch my nose and the beautiful buds will

2

unfurl and springtime will have arrived in Misty Wood at last!"

Bailey the Bud Bunny sat at the old log that was her family's breakfast table, chattering away. She was so excited that her pretty pink wings kept fluttering and she had to

3

hold on to the table to stop herself from flying off. Bailey's mom was bustling about the warm burrow. Her dad was busy tweaking his whiskers and arranging his long floppy ears. And her baby brother,

Bobby, was sitting on his toadstool
high chair, playing with his mashed
carrots. Bailey leaned across the
log table and put her little pink
nose close to Bobby's face.

"I'll twitch my nose like this,

Bobby," she said, wiggling her nose slowly. "I have to be careful because the petals are very delicate. If I do it too quickly, the flower might break. Ouch!" she yelped as Bobby whacked the tip of her nose with his little white paw.

"Bweak! Bweak!" the baby bunny cried.

Bailey laughed. "When you're a bigger Bud Bunny, you'll understand." She fluttered her tiny

6

pink wings proudly. Like all the fairy animals living in Misty Wood, she had a very special job to do to make sure it stayed such a magical place.

A Bud Bunny's special job was to unfurl the flowers and reveal their beautiful blooms. Bailey was a very young Bud Bunny and this was only her second springtime. Her white cotton tail fluffed up with happiness as she thought back to last year. All the other Bud Bunnies

had said she'd done really well.
This year she was determined to do
even better.

And maybe if I'm really good,
Bailey thought, *I might even see
the Easter Bunny at the Misty Wood
Easter Egg Hunt.* Her mom always
said that no one got to meet the
Easter Bunny, because he was so
busy and important. But Bailey
still hoped that, one day, she'd be
really lucky.

"I'm sure I'll see all sorts of lovely flowers today," Bailey said dreamily. "Big ones and small ones. Pink ones and blue ones. Short ones and tall ones and some in-between ones and . . ."

"Bailey, if you don't stop chattering and finish up your food, it will be time for bed before you've even started," her mom said, stirring a wooden pot of fresh elderflower juice.

"Sorry," Bailey said with a grin. "I'm just so happy. I've been waiting for today *forever*!"

Her mom set the pot down on the log table. "Well, you can wait just a little bit longer and have a nice big drink first. It's a lovely sunny day outside and I don't want you getting thirsty." She poured some of the sweet juice into Bailey's acorn cup and the little bunny gulped it eagerly.

"Yum, that was delicious," she said, licking her lips. "Now, I can't hang around. I've got to hurry,

hurry, hurry—*hic!*" Bailey stopped, openmouthed.

Bobby giggled.

Bailey's mom gasped.

Bailey's dad raised an eyebrow.

Bailey tried again.

"Good-bye, everyone," she said. "I'm off to—*hic!*" She stopped and looked around the burrow in dismay. "What's—*hic*—happening?" she wailed.

"Oh, Bailey," her mom said,

12

shaking her head. "You drank
your juice so quickly, it's given you
the hiccups."

"Hiccups?" Bailey cried. "But

13

how am I—*hic*—going to do my—*hic*—job now? I'll never be able to keep still enough to unfurl the flower petals if I've got the—*hic*—hiccups!"

And, with that, a fat tear trickled down her snowy-white face and landed—*splat!*—into her empty acorn cup.

CHAPTER TWO

The Cheeky Pollen Puppy

"Cheer up," Bailey's dad said. He hopped over and patted her on the head with one of his big, furry

paws. "Hiccups don't last forever. Once you're flying around outside, they'll soon disappear."

"Really—*hic*—truly?" Bailey said hopefully.

"Really truly," her dad replied.

"Dad's right," Bailey's mom said. "The fresh air is sure to get rid of your hiccups."

Bailey glanced at the dandelion clock on the wall.

"Ooh," she squeaked when she

saw the time blowing away. "I'd better go. I've got buds to—*hic*—unfurl."

She said a hasty and hiccupy good-bye to her family and set off through the Misty Wood Rabbit Warren. As she scampered along the tunnels, she passed the homes of the other Bud Bunnies. Many of them were getting ready to go out and unfurl the flowers, too, so there was lots of hustle and bustle.

"Isn't it exciting, Bailey? Springtime at last!" a little gray bunny called out, twitching his floppy ears. It was Ben, one of Bailey's best friends.

"Hello, Ben!" Bailey said with a smile. "Yes, it's really exciting—*hic*. Oh no, not again!" Bailey covered her mouth with her paw.

"Oh, Bailey," Ben said, looking worried. "Was that a hiccup?"

"Yes." Bailey sighed. "Of all the

18

mornings to get them, why did it
have to be this one?"

"That *is* bad luck." Ben tipped

his head to one side thoughtfully.
"But I'm sure they'll disappear
when you get outside. Mom
says fresh air and sunshine cure
everything."

"I hope she's right," Bailey
said. "See you up there, then, Ben—
hic!"

Ben grinned at her and waved
good-bye.

Bailey turned the corner and
saw a bright yellow glow at the

end of the tunnel ahead of her.
She scampered toward it and
emerged, blinking, into the golden
spring sunshine of Misty Wood.
As her eyes grew used to the light,
she gasped in delight. Spread out
before her was Honeydew Meadow.
Its bright green grass was carpeted
with new flowers, all tightly closed
and waiting for the Bud Bunnies to
open them.

Bailey could see the other

Bud Bunnies already setting to work. As they twitched their noses and each bud unfurled, beautiful splashes of color burst out. Bailey couldn't wait to join in. She flew over to the nearest stem and

placed her nose against its delicate
bud. Slowly, carefully, she got
ready to twitch her nose and . . .

"*Hic!*"

Bailey jumped backward in
surprise, knocking the bud away.

"Oh no!" she sighed. *Perhaps I need some more fresh air*, she thought. She took a deep breath. Then she carefully put her nose back to the flower.

"*Hic*—no!" she cried as her nose jerked and bumped the bud away again. "What am I going to—*hic*—do?"

The sound of laughter rang out across the meadow. Bailey turned to see where it was coming from.

There, on a grassy bank behind
her, was a little Pollen Puppy. He
was chuckling so hard his golden
wings were jiggling up and down.

"You looked so funny," he cried

merrily. "Do it again, do it again! Please!"

Bailey folded her paws and glared at him. Like all the fairy animals in Misty Wood, Pollen Puppies had an important job to do—spreading the golden pollen in the meadows and fields so the flowers could grow. But they were also very cheeky and loved to joke around.

"I'm not doing it on purpose,

you know," Bailey said. She felt quite annoyed. "I've got the—*hic*—hiccups."

"The hic-hiccups?" the puppy repeated, and burst out laughing again. "Those are just the funniest hiccups I've ever seen."

"Well, I don't think they're funny," Bailey said. "And neither will the rest of Misty Wood if I can't get these buds open and looking pretty." She slumped

down in the long grass and began to cry.

The Pollen Puppy stopped laughing immediately. "I'm very sorry," he said quickly. "I didn't mean to upset you."

He scampered over to Bailey and patted her on the back. Although Pollen Puppies were mischievous, they were very kind fairy animals at heart.

"Look, don't cry," he said. "I think

I know how you can get rid of your hiccups."

"*Hic*—really?" Bailey gave a small sniff and wiped her eyes.

"*Hic*—really." The puppy smiled. "Follow me."

CHAPTER THREE
Head Over Heels

"My name's Petey, by the way," the puppy called back over his golden wings as they flew up into the warm air. "What's yours?"

"Bailey," she replied. She fluttered her wings faster to keep up, but it wasn't easy to fly when you had the hiccups. Every time she hiccuped she fell a bit behind.

Finally, they reached a clearing. Down below them was a huge pond. It glistened silver and blue in the sunlight.

"Moonshine Pond!" exclaimed Bailey, looking down. "What are we doing here?"

Petey guided her down gently to the sandy shore of the pond. "To get rid of hiccups, you need to have a drink," he explained.

"A drink?" Bailey shook her head. "Oh, no. It was drinking juice that *gave* me the hiccups. I don't think I ought to—*hic*—drink any more."

Petey grinned. "Ah, but you got the hiccups from drinking *forward*," he explained. "So to get rid of them, you have to do the opposite. You have to drink *backward*."

Bailey was confused. "Drink

backward? How am I supposed to drink backward?"

Petey shrugged his shoulders. "I'm not exactly sure," he said. "I heard my grandma say it to my sister once when she had the hiccups. It must have worked because she hasn't had them since. Come on!"

Bailey watched as Petey dashed down to the edge of the pond, where the pearly water lapped over silver pebbles.

"It does look really nice,"
Bailey said, hopping after Petey.
"Perhaps it will do the—*hic*—trick."
She leaned forward to take a slurp
of the sparkling water.

"No, not like that!" Petey cried.

Bailey froze. "What's the—*hic*—
matter?" she asked.

"You have to drink backward,
remember?" Petey said. "Look, I
think it's like this."

He put his paws on her back

35

and turned her around so that she was facing away from the pond. "Now," he said, "lean backward and take a drink."

"Lean backward?" Bailey shook her head. "But that's—*hic*—impossible."

"Do you want to get rid of your hiccups or not?" Petey asked.

Bailey gave a sigh and bent backward until the tips of her ears dangled down into the water.

"Brrr. The water's cold!" she squeaked. But then she hiccuped again. She leaned back even farther, so that the top of her head was in the water and her furry tummy was pointing up to the sky.

"Nearly there," Petey called out cheerily. "You'll soon have gotten rid of those—uh-oh—oh no— oh, dear!"

SPLASH!

Bailey had lost her balance.

She tumbled head over heels
into the water and landed with a
splishy sploshy PLOP,
right on her bottom.

"Ow, ow, ow!" she cried, clambering out of the pond. She shook the water from her whiskers and at the same time let out an enormous . . .

"*HICCUP!*"

Petey rolled around on the bank of Moonshine Pond, laughing and laughing.

"You looked so funny!" he gasped. "Do it again! Please!"

"Stop—*hic*—saying that!"

39

Bailey thumped her furry white foot. "You said you would help me get rid of my hiccups—*HIC*—but now they're even—*HIC*—worse than before. And I'm soaking wet!"

She stretched out her poor bedraggled wings.

"Sorry," Petey said again. "But it really wasn't my fault. Honestly, Bailey, it can't be that hard to drink backward."

"Okay, then," Bailey said. "If

you think it's so easy, why don't you—*HIC*—try it?"

Petey clapped his front paws together and grinned. "All right, little Bud Bunny. I'll show you how it's done."

Petey marched down to the edge of the pond. Then he turned around and set his back legs wide apart. Slowly, he bent backward, tipping his soft, furry head down toward the water.

"See how easy it is?" he said.

"Look, I'm nearly there."

But just at that moment, his legs began to wobble. "Just a little bit farther," he gasped. "Whoa!"

There was an almighty

SPLASH

and this time it was Petey who tumbled, head over heels, into the cold water.

Now it was

Bailey's turn to laugh. "You looked so funny!" she cried. "Like a big golden frog hopping off a lily pad!"

Petey bounded out of the pond, shaking his fur and sending water spraying in all directions.

"I suppose it serves me right," he said with a chuckle. He flopped down on the grass beside Bailey. "Now we're both soaking.

Drinking backward isn't as easy as I thought."

"No, it's not," Bailey said, her smile fading. "So, what am I going to do now?"

CHAPTER FOUR

The Best Cure for Hiccups Ever

Bailey and Petey stretched out

on the bank. The sun felt lovely

and warm on their damp fur,

and they soon began to dry out.

Bailey was still hiccuping, though. "Today has been the unluckiest day of my life," she sighed. "I've been looking forward to unfurling the flowers for a whole year, but at this rate I won't be able to open a single— *hic*—bud."

Just at that moment, there was a rustle in the hedgerow behind them. A small black face with a

pointy nose and tiny eyes peered at them grumpily.

"Hey, what's going on out there?" the creature said crossly. "All your noise woke me up."

"Oh no, it's—*hic*—Marley," Bailey whispered to Petey.

"*Hic*—who?" Petey whispered back.

"Marley the Moonbeam Mole," Bailey explained. "He's a—*hic*—friend of my mom and

47

dad's. We're in big trouble now."

Marley squeezed his velvety

little body out of his hiding place.

He shook out his glittery wings and made his way toward them.

"He doesn't look very happy," Petey whispered.

"Of course he's not," Bailey said. "Moonbeam Moles sleep during the day because they— *hic*—have to work all night."

"Of course," Petey said. "They catch the moonbeams to put in the pond to make it all shimmery."

"Exactly." Bailey nodded.

"So, right now, Marley should be fast asleep."

"Bailey, is that you?" Marley's tiny eyes blinked blindly.

"Hello, Marley. Yes, it's me," said Bailey.

The sleepy mole's velvety brow furrowed. "What are you doing all the way over here? It's the first day of spring. Shouldn't you be busy in the meadow opening the buds?"

"She was," Petey quickly

explained. "I was the one who brought her here. Sorry."

"So you should be, young Pollen Puppy," Marley grumbled. "How am I supposed to sleep with all of your chatting and splashing going on?"

"We're so sorry, Marley," Bailey said quickly. "We didn't mean to— *hic*—wake you. *HIC!*"

"Goodness me," Marley gasped. "Those hiccups sound serious."

"They are," Bailey said glumly. "I've had them all morning and I haven't been able to open a—*hic*—single flower."

"I thought drinking backward might cure them," Petey added. "So that's why we came to your pond."

Marley shook his head and gave a little chuckle. "I've heard of that old cure," he said. "I'm not sure it works every time. But don't worry, I have a much better idea."

"You do?" Bailey and Petey cried.

"Yes, I do. Now listen carefully."
Marley beckoned them closer with
his little pink paw. "What I am
about to tell you is the best cure
for hiccups ever invented."

"It is?" Bailey exclaimed. She
and Petey leaned in eagerly.

"To get rid of hiccups," Marley whispered, "you need to be surprised by something *so* surprising that your hiccups forget to hiccup."

Bailey and Petey looked at each other. "Something *so* surprising that your hiccups forget to hiccup," Bailey repeated. "But I've already done so many surprising things today, Marley. Getting hiccups in the first place

was surprising. Meeting Petey was surprising. And falling into the water was definitely—*hic*—surprising!"

Petey shook his golden head. "Those things can't have been surprising enough," he said.

"Exactly." Marley nodded. "But I'm sure something will come along that you really weren't expecting." Then he gave a big yawn and stretched out his arms.

"I'm afraid I'm very sleepy. So if you don't mind, I will leave you to find the cure by yourselves. Good luck. And good night!"

"Good—*hic*—night," Bailey said. "And thank you, Marley—*hic*!"

As Bailey watched Marley shuffle off to his bed, Petey somersaulted past her, wagging his tail.

"What are you doing, Petey?" Bailey laughed.

"Trying to surprise the hiccups out of you," Petey said, standing up and catching his breath. "Did it work?"

"I don't—*hic*—think so," Bailey said.

"Hmm." Petey scratched his head. With a sudden whoop and twirl, he flew up into the air and performed a series of loop-the-loops in the clear blue sky.

"Any good?" he called.

"*Hic*—no, sorry," Bailey called back. "But it is making me dizzy just looking at you." She closed her eyes for a moment to get rid of the dizziness.

When she opened them again, Petey had completely disappeared. Bailey spun this way and that, trying to catch a glimpse of the little Pollen Puppy, but he was nowhere to be seen.

"Where—*hic*—are you?" Bailey called.

"Boo!" Petey cried, jumping out from behind a clump of clover.

Bailey let out a little squeal and fell backward, landing on her fluffy tail. "Petey, what are you doing?" she said.

"I'm still trying to surprise you." Petey shook the leaves from his ears and bounded over to her. "Is it working?"

"I don't—*hic*—think so, but thank you for trying so hard."

Bailey slumped to the ground in despair. "I've tried fresh air and sunshine and drinking backward and being surprised. But nothing seems to work. I'm beginning to think I'll have these—*hic*—hiccups for—*hic*—ever!"

CHAPTER FIVE

Gee Whiskers!

Bailey's silky ears flopped down over her face. She felt very miserable indeed.

"Don't give up," Petey said,

sitting down in front of her. "Misty Wood is full of helpful fairy animals. Sooner or later we're bound to meet someone who *really* knows how to cure your hiccups."

"Do you—*hic*—think so?" Bailey lifted her little pink nose and tried to smile.

"Yes, I do," Petey replied firmly. "Why don't we go a little farther into the woods, and see who we can find?"

"Okay," Bailey said, nodding her soft white head. "And while we fly, I'm going to take lots of deep breaths of fresh air."

"Good plan," Petey grinned. "Come on, follow me!"

He flicked his wings and took off into the sky, with Bailey close behind. This time they swooped low over Misty Wood, hoping to catch a glimpse of someone else who could help them.

As she flew over Heather Hill, Bailey breathed in the delicious scent of the purple heather. But that didn't cure her hiccups.

In Bluebell Glade, they played chase with the butterflies. But that didn't cure her hiccups, either.

As they flew, Bailey noticed the hard work her fellow Bud Bunnies had done. Lots of flowers had been opened, making Misty Wood look like a brightly colored patchwork

quilt. How she wished she could join the other bunnies!

Next, they flew toward a sunny clearing. Even here there were hundreds of new buds just waiting to be opened.

"Please can we land?" Bailey asked. She couldn't help wanting to take a closer peep. "Oh, Petey," she sighed as they landed in the springy grass. "I should—*hic*—be unfurling these buds."

"And you will be soon," Petey said. "I just know it."

"I hope so," Bailey said. "Because I'm starting to get very tired and my wings have gone all

68

droopy. It's hard work having the hiccups, you know."

Just then, the glinting sunlight on the grass faded and darkness fell over the clearing.

"Is it nighttime already?" Bailey exclaimed.

"No," Petey replied. "It's a shadow. And it's coming from that huge creature over there."

They both looked up to see a massive figure coming slowly

toward them through the woods. Its face was covered in darkness, but the shadow it cast was very big.

"Who do you think it is?" Petey whispered, grabbing Bailey by the paw.

"I don't know," Bailey said. "It's very big—maybe it's a giraffe."

"But giraffes don't live in Misty Wood!" Petey pulled Bailey behind a bush.

"Who's there?" the big

shadowy figure called in a deep voice.

"Maybe it's an elephant?" Bailey whispered.

Petey shook his head. "Elephants don't live here, either."

"I said, who's there?" the voice boomed again.

Petey put his paw to his mouth, signaling to Bailey to keep quiet. Bailey nodded, but as she did so, she let out an enormous . . .

"HICCUP!"

72

GEE WHISKERS!

At once the footsteps began *thump thump thump*ing toward the bush.

"I know someone's there," the voice called again.

Petey and Bailey exchanged glances.

"I bet you two hazelnut buns it's a tiger!" Petey whispered.

THUD.

The footsteps came closer.

"With really big feet!" Petey hissed again.

THUMP.

The ground around them began to shake.

"And a really huge body!" Petey continued.

SWISH!

SWOOSH!

The bush began to rustle.

"And a really long tail," Petey finished.

"But—*hic*—tigers don't live here, either!" Bailey gasped.

"Come out!" the voice boomed, very, very close now.

Bailey and Petey looked at each other.

Bailey took a deep breath, and forgetting about her hiccups, decided to be brave. "I bet you two

hazelnut buns it *isn't* a tiger!" she said, and peeped out from behind the bush.

"Gee whiskers!" she cried in astonishment. "I can't believe it's you!"

CHAPTER SIX

A Surprise So Surprising . . .

"Who is it? Who is it?" Petey

whispered from his hiding place.

But Bailey was so surprised

that she couldn't answer him right away.

"Is it a tiger with really big feet and a really huge body and a really long tail?" Petey asked.

"No!" Bailey cried in delight. "It's—it's the Easter Bunny!"

Petey came bounding out from behind the bush. "The Easter Bunny?" he yapped excitedly. "Are you sure?"

The fairy animal friends both

rubbed their eyes with their paws and looked again. Sure enough, towering over them was a very large white bunny. He had a bright pink nose, pointy ears, and long, feathery whiskers. In his front paws he held a huge basket of brightly colored eggs.

"Oh, Mister Easter Bunny, sir," Bailey cried. "I'm so pleased to meet you. You are my hero! You are my favorite bunny in the

80

whole wide world—apart from my
mom and dad and baby brother,
Bobby, of course. Oh, and my
grandma and grandpa and great-
uncle Boris. And my cousin Bella."
Bailey grinned. "But after all of
them, you're my favorite bunny
for sure! The eggs you bring are
so delicious, and it's so much fun
trying to find them." She took a
hop backward and gazed up at the
huge Easter Bunny. "I can't believe

I've met you. I always hoped, but I never dreamed I'd actually be so lucky!" Bailey tilted her head to one side.

"But why are you here? It's only the first day of spring. Easter isn't for ages. Oh, this is so exciting, isn't it, Petey?" Bailey turned to

Petey and clapped her paws.

Petey just kept on grinning.

"Well, you certainly are a talkative little Bud Bunny," the Easter Bunny said, smiling down at Bailey. "But I'm afraid I can't stop for long because I am in the middle of a very important job."

"Ooh, what is it?" Bailey cried.

The Easter Bunny bent right down so that he could whisper in her ear. "The reason I am here,

84

little Bud Bunny, is to *practice* hiding eggs for the Misty Wood Easter Egg Hunt."

"Practice?" Bailey's eyes opened wide.

The Easter Bunny nodded. "How do you think I get so good at hiding them?"

"That's just like me opening the flowers with my nose," Bailey said. "It takes a lot of practice to get it right." She looked down at

85

the ground and her fluffy white ears flopped over her face. "But I haven't gotten *any* right this year."

The Easter Bunny put down his basket of eggs. "Why ever not?"

"Something awful has happened," Bailey said sadly. "I've got the worst case of hiccups ever. Lots of fairy animals have tried to help me cure them, but nothing has worked. Petey and I were looking for someone else who might be able to help."

"I think—" Petey began.

But Bailey hadn't finished.

"Mr. Easter Bunny, sir, you've reminded me that the wood always looks so pretty when we have the Misty Wood Easter Egg Hunt."

"I think—" Petey said again, but Bailey kept talking.

"But this year," she said, sniffing miserably, "it's not going to look *nearly* so pretty because I haven't been able to help unfurl all the buds. Oh, dear, I don't—"

"Shh!" The Easter Bunny held

up a big paw and Bailey stopped

talking at once.

"Do you realize," the Easter

Bunny said in his kindly voice,

"that you haven't hiccuped once

since you've been talking to me?

I think, my dear Bud Bunny, that

your hiccups might finally be

cured!"

"That's what I've been trying

to say!" Petey said with a giggle.

Bailey clapped her paws with

glee. "You're right!" She paused and swallowed hard a few times. "I don't feel hiccupy at all." She fluttered her pink wings and fluffed up her whiskers. Then she turned to Petey. "Marley the Moonbeam Mole was right after all. I *have* been surprised by something so surprising that my hiccups have forgotten to hiccup!"

CHAPTER SEVEN

Hic, Hic, Hooray!

Bailey was so happy that she did a little hop in the air, landing right at the Easter Bunny's feet. "Thank you, thank you, thank you!" she cried

excitedly. "You are the best surprise *ever*!"

The Easter Bunny chuckled. "I'm very glad to hear it," he said.

Bailey did another bunny hop. "Oh, Easter Bunny. Is there anything I can do to repay you for curing my hiccups?"

The Easter Bunny smiled down at Bailey. "Well," he began, "it just so happens that there *is* something you could do. Both of you, in fact." He turned to look at Petey, too.

"Oh, yes." The little puppy wagged his tail eagerly. "Anything at all."

93

The Easter Bunny tweaked his whiskers thoughtfully. "Well, as I told you, I'm here to do a very important job—practicing hiding the eggs for the Easter Egg Hunt."

"Yes! Yes!" Petey said, chasing his tail with excitement.

"But how can I tell if I've hidden them really well, unless I have some helpers trying to find them?" the Easter Bunny said, his eyes twinkling.

A huge smile spread across Bailey's face. "You mean, you'd like *us* to try and find them?"

The Easter Bunny nodded. "If you would be so kind."

"Gee whiskers! That is the best job ever!" Bailey exclaimed.

Petey rolled onto his back and waved his paws in the air with delight.

"So you'll do it?" the Easter Bunny said.

"Yes!" Bailey and Petey cried at the tops of their voices.

"Thank you," the Easter Bunny said warmly. "Well, first of all, I

need you to close your eyes while I hide two eggs. And no peeking!"

"We won't," Bailey said. She closed her eyes tightly and listened to the rustling of leaves as the Easter Bunny set about hiding the eggs.

"All right, you can open them now," the Easter Bunny called.

"This is so much fun!" Petey said as they started flying around looking for the eggs.

Bailey looked under bushes and on top of branches.

Petey looked behind stones and inside nests.

The Easter Bunny leaned against an oak tree and watched as they searched high and low. "It looks as if I have done a most excellent job," he said.

Bailey was just about to give up when she caught a glimpse of something shimmering behind a

lavender bush. Very carefully, she reached a paw inside the bush and pulled out a beautiful pink speckled egg. "It matches my wings!" She beamed.

The Easter Bunny chuckled. "So it does."

Across the clearing, Petey pulled a chocolate egg from a hollow tree trunk and let out a cheer. "I found one, too!" he cried.

Bailey and Petey flew over

to the Easter Bunny with their beautiful eggs.

"Well done," he said, smiling down at them.

"I didn't think we were ever going to find them," Bailey said.

"So you don't think I need any more practice at hiding them?" the Easter Bunny said.

Bailey shook her head. "No! You're the world's best hider ever."

She went to put the beautiful

HIC, HIC, HOORAY!

pink egg back in his basket, but the Easter Bunny put a fluffy white paw out. "You can keep it," he said. "After all, it does match your wings."

"Can I keep mine?" Petey asked, looking longingly at the chocolate egg. "It matches my paws . . . sort of."

The Easter Bunny nodded. "In that case, you must."

Bailey licked the pink egg. It tasted delicious, like spun sugar.

Petey took a bite from his

chocolate egg. "Yum!" he said, licking his lips.

The Easter Bunny watched, smiling as they gobbled up their eggs. "Well, now I must be off," he said when they'd finished.

"Already?" Bailey said.

The Easter Bunny picked up his basket. "I'm afraid so. But don't forget, you have something else to do now your hiccups have gone," he grinned as he waved good-bye.

Bailey put her paw to her mouth. "My buds!" she cried.

"Come on, Petey, we need to get going. Good-bye, Mr. Easter Bunny, sir, and thank you!"

With a last wave, the Easter Bunny hopped off into Misty Wood and Bailey and Petey took to the sky once more. They flew swiftly to Honeydew Meadow, where Bailey's buds were still waiting to be opened.

"Here goes," Bailey muttered

as she landed next to an unfurled flower. "Wish me luck, Petey."

"Good luck, Bailey," whispered Petey.

Cautiously, Bailey shuffled up to the nearest flower.

Very slowly, she put her tiny pink nose to the tightly furled bud.

She waited for just a moment. Had her hiccups really gone? Would she be able to keep still for long enough?

105

She placed her nose gently against the delicate petals, and twitched. At first, nothing happened. Then, slowly, the petals started to unfurl. Bailey gasped as the flower burst into life.

Each petal was as soft as satin and as bright as a jewel. She had never seen anything quite so pretty.

"I did it, I did it!" squeaked Bailey, hopping back to admire her handiwork.

Petey cheered and clapped. "I knew you could," he cried, "once you got rid of those hiccups."

"Well, I'm very glad they've gone, Petey," she said. "But I'm also very glad I had them."

"Really? But why?" Petey asked.

Bailey beamed at him. "Because if I hadn't gotten the hiccups, I would never have met you. And you would never have agreed to help me. And we would never have gone all

over Misty Wood searching for a cure.
And we would never have found the
Easter Bunny.

"So, you see, I made a new friend
and got to meet my hero all in one
day. And all because of the hiccups!"

Petey did a little flip of joy.
"In that case, I say three cheers for
hiccups!"

"I agree!" Bailey cried. "Hic, hic,
hooray!"

Turn the page for
lots of fun
Misty Wood
activities!

Connect the Dots

Follow the numbers and connect all
the dots to make a lovely picture from
the story.

Start with dot number 1. When you've
finished connecting all the dots, you can
color the picture in!

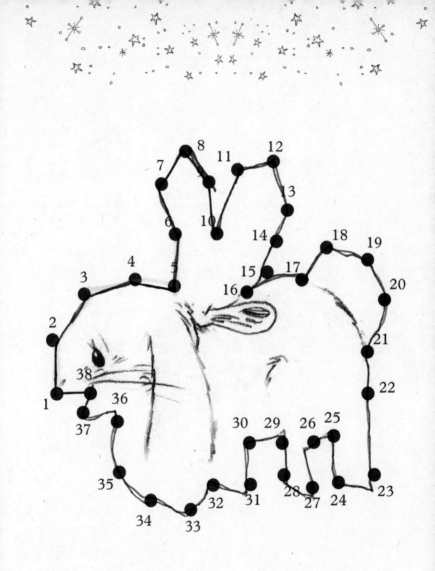

Help Bailey and Petey
find their Easter eggs!

Draw your own brightly
colored Easter eggs to go
in Bailey's basket!

Spring Is Spectacular!

Bailey's favorite things about springtime are the flower buds that bloom into sweet spring blossoms. She loves big ones and small ones, pink ones and blue ones!

What are your favorite springtime flowers? Write them down below and draw a picture of each one in the boxes on the next page.

1. ~~sunflower~~ *sunflower* *sunflower*

2. ~~lily~~ *lily*

3. ~~begonia~~ *bataunia*

Nice
work
for
this

Misty Wood Word Search

Use the words below to create your own word search! Write all the words in the boxes, then fill the other spaces with lots of different letters. See if a friend can solve it!

LAVENDER
WHISKERS
ACORN
PETALS
HICCUP
EASTER
SUNLIGHT
SPLASH
BUTTERFLY

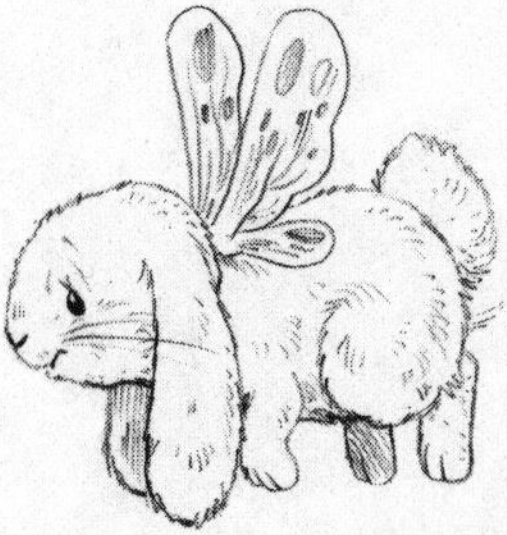

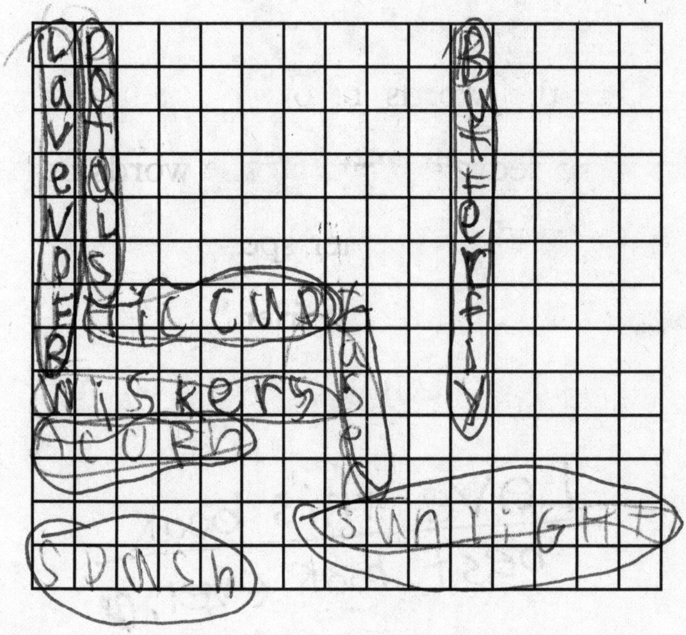

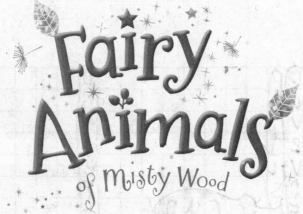

Fairy Animals
of misty Wood

Meet more Fairy Animal friends!

Love this book
best book ever. ♥

Fun
activities
inside!

Chloe
the Kitten

Fairy
Animals
of Misty Wood

Lily Small

Fun
activities
inside!

Bella
the Bunny

Fairy
Animals
of Misty Wood

Lily Small

Fun
activities
inside!

Paddy
the Puppy

Fairy
Animals
of Misty Wood

Lily Small

Fun
activities
inside!

Mia
the Mouse

Fairy
Animals
of Misty Wood

Lily Small

Fun
Activities
inside!

Kylie
the
Kitten

Fairy
Animals
of Misty Wood

Lily Small

Fun
Activities
inside!

Paige
the Pony

Fairy
Animals
of Misty Wood

Lily Small

Fun
Activities
inside!

Penny
the Puppy

Fairy
Animals
of Misty Wood

Lily Small

Fun
Activities
inside!

Bailey
the Bunny

Fairy
Animals
of Misty Wood

Lily Small